TOO MANY TURNERS

by Wendy Wax
illustrated by Harry Moore

SCHOLASTIC INC.

New York Toronto London Auckland Sydney
Mexico City New Delhi Hong Kong Buenos Aires

Based on the TV series *The Fairly OddParents*®
created by Butch Hartman as seen on Nickelodeon®

ISBN 0-439-66669-4

4 5 6 7 8 9/0

12 11 10 9 8 7 6 5 4 3 2 1   23

Printed in the U.S.A.

First Scholastic printing, November 2004

Nelvana is the International Representative. NELVANA® Nelvana Limited CORUS™
Corus Entertainment Inc.

It was Saturday. Timmy Turner
had the whole day ahead of him.
After breakfast he set out for
Chester's house.

Chester was making lemonade.

"Hey, Chester," Timmy said.

"Want to go to the park?"

"I can't," said Chester.

"We are having a family reunion.

One hundred relatives
are coming over.
Thirty-four are already here."
"Wow!" said Timmy.

Timmy went to A.J.'s house.

A.J. was on his bike.

"Want to go to the park?"

Timmy asked.

"I can't," said A.J. "We are going

on a family bike ride and then

watching family movies."

"Too bad," said Timmy.

nt home. "Can we have a

he asked his parents.

Mr. Turner.

going to our 'Spending

Saturdays with Your Child' class."

"So we will know how to spend time with you!" said Mrs. Turner. "Vicky is coming to babysit."

Timmy groaned.

Timmy tried playing alone,
but it was no fun.
He tried working on his
monster robot, but the eyes
would not light up.

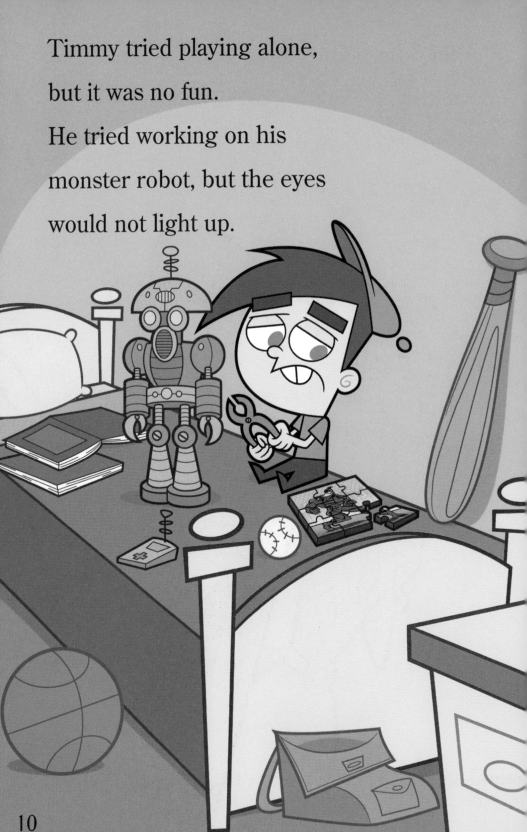

"You look bored," said Cosmo.

"Are you okay?" Wanda asked.

"Being an only child sure is lonely,"
Timmy said to his fairy godparents.

"How can you be lonely with us around all the time?" asked Cosmo. "Yeah, sweetie. You always have us!" added Wanda.

"I know, but I can't play with you anywhere I want to. I have to keep you a secret," said Timmy.

Poof!

"I wish I had lots of brothers and
sisters to play with," Timmy said.
POOF! Cosmo and Wanda made
his wish come true.

13

"Hey, big brother," called a boy.
"Big brother?" said Timmy,
liking the sound of it. He looked
around. Kids of all ages
were everywhere, and they
looked a lot like him.
"Welcome to my family, person
who looks like me!" said Timmy.

One of Timmy's older sisters

inspected his monster robot.

"It will not light up," he told her.

"These wires need to touch,"

said the girl. "Like this."

The robot's eyes lit up.

"Thanks, big sis!" said Timmy.

"Will you read to us?" asked Timmy's little brothers and sisters. "Sure," said Timmy. He found his favorite issue of The Crimson Chin and began to read when . . . CRASH!

The sound came from Timmy's

bedroom. "Oh, no!" he cried.

His robot was broken.

"It was an accident," said a boy

with a tennis racquet.

Timmy saw a baby chewing on his favorite Crimson Chin action figure. "Stop that!" he yelled, but it was no use.

The house was noisy, crowded,
and messy.

"I wish I were an only child
again," Timmy said.

But nothing happened. Timmy looked around for Cosmo and Wanda—but the fishbowl was gone!

Timmy's parents came in.

They looked tired and frazzled.

"Can we borrow some money?"

Mrs. Turner asked Timmy.

"You want to borrow money

from me?" Timmy asked.

"We will need help paying Vicky,"
explained Mr. Turner. "Her
rates went up because of all of
your brothers and sisters."
Sadly, Timmy handed over his
piggy bank.

Timmy went downstairs.

"Hi, Tommy!" Vicky said sweetly.

"It's Timmy," said Timmy. Then he realized Vicky had been talking to his older brother Tommy.

Vicky didn't even try to boss Timmy
around. She didn't read stories
or offer snacks, either.
All she did was try to get
Tommy's attention.
In a weird way, Timmy missed
Vicky's attention.

25

"Cosmo! Wanda!" Timmy shouted,

pushing through a crowd of siblings.

"What?" asked a boy named Cosmo.

"Yes?" asked a girl named Wanda.

"Never mind," Timmy said, sighing.

Upstairs, Timmy found a girl
trying on his mom's makeup.
"Have you seen my fishbowl?"
he asked her. Just then he
heard something in the bathroom.

A set of triplets dangled the fairy
godparents above the toilet.
"Fish are icky!" they said. Cosmo
and Wanda squirmed to get loose.

Timmy grabbed Cosmo and Wanda.

"I wish I were an only child again,"
he said quickly.

Cosmo and Wanda were happy to
grant his wish. POOF!

"Are you lonely without brothers
and sisters to play with?"
Wanda asked.

"Not at all," said Timmy.

"I will never be lonely
with you two around!"

Cosmo and Wanda smiled proudly.

Just then Vicky stormed in.

"It looks like a hurricane hit

this house," she shouted.

"Clean it—NOW!"

"Okay," said Timmy. He didn't

have anything better to do

on this Saturday afternoon.

While Timmy was cleaning,

Chester called.

"My cousins want to meet you,"

he said. "Can you come over?"

"Oh, brother!" said Timmy.

"I'm not in a family sort of mood."

Cosmo screamed. "Please, Timmy!

Don't say the word 'brother'

for a long time!"